STICKER STORIES

We Are Ballerinas

Illustrated by Cathy Beylon

GROSSET & DUNLAP • NEW YORK

We are ballerinas!
We go to dance class.
It's time to get ready.

The music begins.
We start our warm-ups.
Who will be at the *barre* today?

We love getting dressed up for a show!
Pick out things for us to wear.

The maypole dance is fun.
Help us wind our ribbons
around and around!

Now we dance in a winter wonderland.
Can you decorate the stage?

Bright colors fill this candyland scene.
Where are all the other dancers?

The show is over.
The audience claps for us.
Who else takes a bow?

It's party time!
Can you make a great party for us?